PINGU

the Adventurer

BBC CHILDREN'S BOOKS

BUILDING IGLOOS

Pingu was to spend his first night away from home with a friend. They were going to camp outside.

Mum and Dad were a bit anxious. "Put this hat on," said Dad. "You'll be glad of it in the night."

"Take some fish, too," said Mum. "You never know when you'll feel hungry."

"What a fuss!" thought Pingu and hurried off as quickly as he could.

There was his friend Punki waiting for him.
"Hullo," cried Pingu. "I thought I'd never get
away. Mum and Dad made me pack a huge box of
things they thought we'd need in the night."

"There's a pile of ice blocks over there," said Punki. "Shall we make an igloo to spend the night in?"

"What a great idea!" said Pingu.

But the two friends couldn't agree on where to build the igloo.

"The view's better over here," said Pingu.

"But it's much flatter over there," said Punki.

They were both so determined to have their own way that they ended up each building a separate igloo and scowling at each other.

Punki was faster. He'd soon built a whole wall —
but it looked a bit wobbly. Pingu was building his
igloo more slowly and carefully.

There was one block of ice left.

"I need it," cried Pingu.

"No," said Punki. "I got it first."

As the two friends argued, Punki's wall began to tumble down.

And then down came Pingu's wall, too.

"All that work for nothing," sobbed Punki.

"It'll soon be dark and we've nowhere to sleep," said Pingu wearily.

"There's only one thing for it," said Pingu. "We'll
have to build an igloo together."

So the two friends began all over again. It was
much quicker work with two and in no time at all a
perfect little igloo began to take shape.

At last it was finished, just as night fell. Pingu
added the last block and then slid happily down the
roof.

"Now let's see what you've got in your box," said
Punki, pushing Pingu's sledge through the door.

Punki and Pingu unpacked an oil lamp, some
matches, a rug and plenty to eat.

"Your mum and dad think of everything," said
Punki admiringly as he laid the rug out on the floor.

"We've certainly deserved our dinner," said
Pingu, tucking into a large fish.

"You bet!" said Punki.

And the two friends chatted away for half the
night until they both fell happily asleep.

PINGU'S DREAM

One evening, when Pingu was tucked up in bed, Mum read him a story. It was an exciting story about horses, but Pingu was so tired he could hardly keep his eyes open.

Suddenly Pingu sat up. He was sure his bed was starting to move and the picture above him was shaking about.

"Help, help," he cried. "It's an earthquake!"

But nobody heard him.

Then a cold wind came blowing through the
room. It blew so hard that the igloo took off up into
the air, leaving Pingu and his bed behind.
"This can't be happening!" thought Pingu.

Pingu's bed began to rock about, shaking him
forwards and backwards.

"Stop it!" shouted Pingu.

"You won't escape," said the monster in a blood-curdling voice. He picked up Pingu's igloo in one paw as if it was as light as a feather.

"Help, Mum, Mum!" cried Pingu as the monster came closer and closer.

Pingu was so frightened he fell right out of his bed.

"I'm feeling hungry and you'll make a tasty
meal," said the monster.

"Can't anyone help me? What can I do?" cried
Pingu.

While the monster sniggered, Pingu got up and
ran as fast as he could. Behind him he could hear
the monster eating the mattress.

"You won't get away. I'll find you wherever you
go," he roared.

Pingu ran and ran. The bed was fleeing
too. Suddenly Pingu found himself sliding
down a steep slope.

"I'm done for," he thought to himself sadly.

"What's the matter, Pingu?" said Mum. "You were
making such a noise that you woke me up."

Pingu looked around him. "I had a terrible
dream," he explained. "But I'm all right now. In fact
I've never felt happier to be home!"

PINGU'S ICE CAVE

Pingo asked Pingu to come out and play with his new ball.

"Why is it so bouncy?" asked Pingu.

"It's just been blown up," Pingo explained proudly.

"I've caught you at last," said a deep, growly
voice behind Pingu.

Pingu was terrified to see a monster looming up
over the ice.

"Please don't hurt me," stammered Pingu.

As suddenly as the bed had started to gallop, it stopped. Its legs shortened again and the mattress bent up.

"Don't stop!" yelled Pingu, but the bed reared up one last time and then came to a standstill.

Next the bed seemed to change its mind and walked about on its legs. It started to gallop like a horse.

"That's better," said Pingu, beginning to enjoy himself. "I've always wanted to ride a horse."

Pingu was even more surprised when the whole
bed tipped right up on end. His pillow and sheet
were thrown to the ground, but Pingu clung on tight.
"You won't throw me off that easily," he cried.

The ball bounced further and further away until it came to a stop on a loose piece of ice. The two friends went to get it.

"Watch out!" cried Pingo as the ground disappeared beneath them.

Both friends found themselves sliding down into an ice cave.

"How will we ever get out?" asked Pingu.

"The way we came in," said Pingo. But as he spoke a piece of ice fell and blocked the hole.

Pingu and Pingo were terrified. How could they escape from this ice prison? Suddenly Pingu spotted a glimmer of light.

"There must be a hole in the ice. We'd better make our way towards it," he said.

Bravely Pingu climbed upwards, sometimes sliding along the ice.

"Can you hear me?" Pingo called out.

At last he heard Pingu call back, "I've got right up. Will you follow me now?"

The ice cave grew brighter and brighter.

"We're nearly there, Pingo," said Pingu. "We've just got to get up this last bit and then we can get out."

"I know you're right," said Pingo nervously.
"But how can we get across this crevasse without
breaking our necks? Just look down there!"

"We'll have to swing across it on this rope.
Do you want to go first, or shall I?'' asked Pingu.
"We'll never make it,'' sobbed Pingo. "Just
thinking of that crevasse makes me feel giddy!''

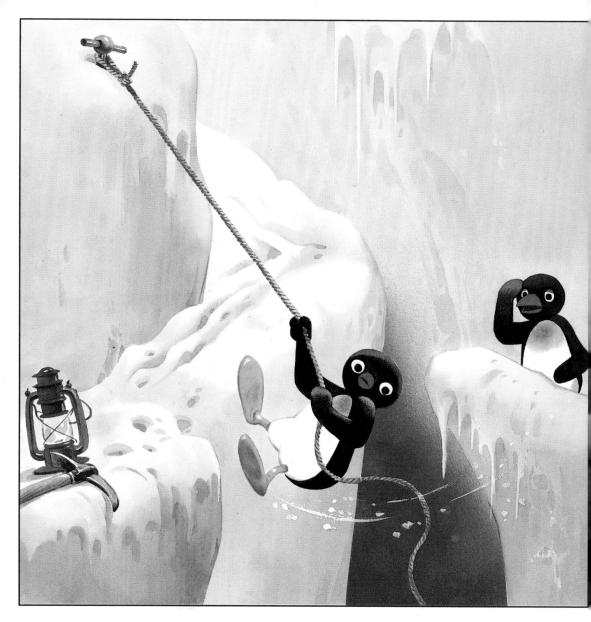

"I'm going to try," said Pingu. He heaved on the
rope and swung across.

"It worked," he shouted happily to Pingo. "Now
it's your turn."

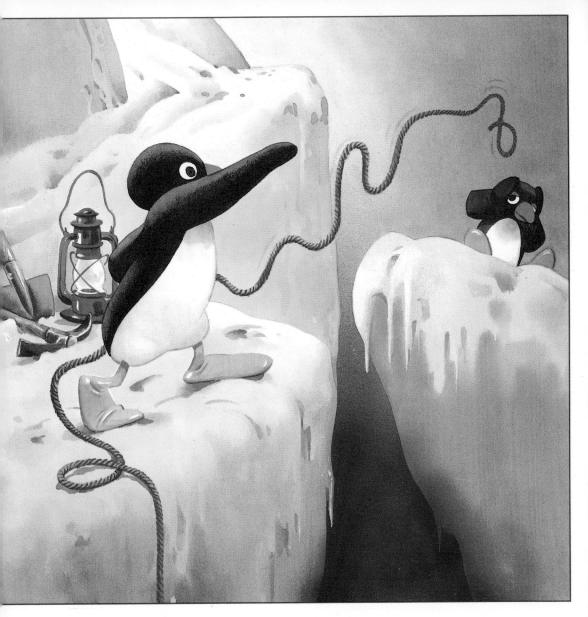

Pingu threw the rope across to Pingo and told him
to fix it on his side.

"Do you think it will hold?" asked Pingo doubtfully.

"Of course it will," said Pingu.

Pingu passed the rope round a huge block of ice at his end and Pingo started to inch his way over the crevasse. He was larger and heavier than Pingu and it took all Pingu's strength to stop him falling into the abyss below.

"We've made it," yelled Pingo when he landed
on his feet. After a short rest the two friends
started on the last steep slope.

"Are we nearly there?" Pingo kept asking.

At last they came out into the fresh air.
"Hurray!" exclaimed Pingo. "We're free."
And the two friends went happily on their way.

Published by BBC Books, a division of BBC Enterprises Limited, Woodlands, 80 Wood Lane, London W12 0TT
First published in Hardback 1991. Illustrations by Tony Wolf. Original text by Sibylle von Flüe.
This edition © BBC Books by arrangement with Dami Editore 1993. Reprinted 1993. Reprinted 1994 (four times).
PINGU © Editory A G Bertschikon 1991. ISBN 0 563 40336 5
Printed and bound in Great Britain by Cambus Litho, East Kilbride